The Teenager Who Came to Tea

THE
TEENAGER
WHO CAME TO TEA

A Parody

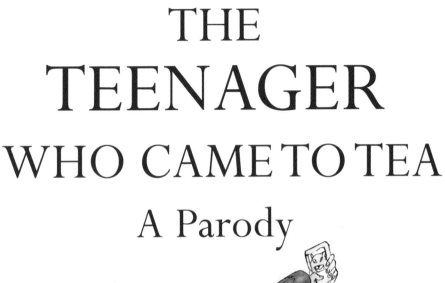

Josie Lloyd & Emlyn Rees
Illustrated by Gillian Johnson

CONSTABLE • LONDON

CONSTABLE

First published in Great Britain in 2015 by Constable

5 7 9 10 8 6

A CIP catalogue record for this book
is available from the British Library.

ISBN: 978-1-4721-2176-9

Page design by Design23
Printed and bound in Italy by
L.E.G.O. SpA

Constable
An imprint of
Little, Brown Book Group
Carmelite House
50 Victoria Embankment
London EC4Y 0DZ

An Hachette UK Company
www.hachette.co.uk

www.littlebrown.co.uk

To all the wonderful teenagers in our lives,
for putting up with us.

Sophie and her daddy were busy making tea,
in their tasteful side return kitchen,
     when all of a sudden, the doorbell rang.

Daddy asked Sophie,
'Who on earth do you think
that could be?'

'There's no way it's the
milkman, because he hasn't
delivered since 1983.

'And it can't be the Ocado van,
because they came this
morning.

'And it can't be Mummy,
because she's the main breadwinner,
and is a kickass corporate lawyer in the City…

'Let's see who it can be.'

Sophie looked
outside and
saw her
big, scruffy
teenage
brother, just
back from
college.

'Alright,
squirt,' he
said, ruffling
her hair.

And Daddy asked, 'How was your day?'

But the teenager pushed past him saying,
'YeahlikewhateverImstarvingOK?'

In the kitchen, Sophie's daddy said,
'Would you like some of the rustic olive
focaccia I just baked?'

But the teenager was already rifling through the
cupboard and said,
   'NahImhavingBarbecuePringlesalright.'

He didn't just eat one handful of Pringles though, he took a selfie of himself pouring a whole tube of them into his mouth, before sending it to his best mate, along with the letters LOL!

His stomach was still growling, so Sophie's daddy offered him a bowl of quinoa, rocket and heritage tomato salad.

But the teenager ignored him. He was too busy crying with laughter, watching an epic fail of a kitten falling off a curtain.

Sophie's daddy said,
'Would you like a glass of organic, lactose-free soya milk?'

But the teenager had already helped himself to a bottle of Diet Coke,

and went into the garden and jammed ten Mentos into it, before filming it bouncing over the neighbour's roof and posting the footage on Vine.

He then came back into the kitchen to see what else he could find.

Before Sophie and
Daddy had a chance to stop him,
he'd poured Daddy's three-day bone-
broth stock-reduction away because,
'Ithoughtitwaswashingupitsmeltwellrank.'

Sophie then watched as he tore a packet of noodles open with his teeth and ate them straight from the pan before gobbling up a whole jar of Nutella with a spoon. . .

. . . and sneaking four bottles of Daddy's Icelandic, glacier-filtered craft lager out of the fridge and into his bag.

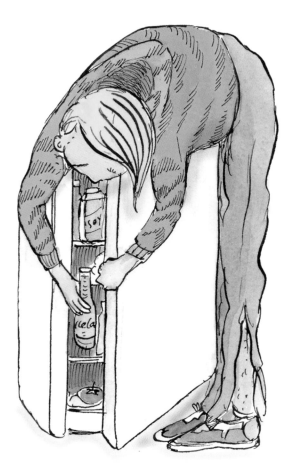

He then said, 'Imgoingforashowerwheresmy-
jeansandcanIborrowsomecash?'

Two hours later, he came back downstairs and said, 'LaterImrevisingatTims.'

'Didn't you say it was football practice with Dave?' Daddy asked.

And the teenager rolled his eyes twice and told him,

'YeahthatswhatIjustsaid.'

Sophie's daddy said, 'I don't know what to do. I've got nothing for Mummy's supper. My oxtail ragout simply won't work without that stock.'

'And he's used up all the hot
water, so you can't have a bath.'

Just then Sophie's mummy came home.
She said, 'Bastard trains. I'm knackered.
What's for dinner?'

So Sophie and Daddy explained what had happened, about how the teenager had ruined Daddy's ragout and pilfered all his booze.

And Sophie's mummy said,
'I know. Let's go to Nando's instead.'

So they went out into the night, and all the
takeaway signs were glowing, and all the cars
were thumping out bass, as they walked down
the road.

And they had a lovely supper of Churrasco
thigh burgers, Halloumi cheese and
Peri-Peri chips.

The next day Sophie and her daddy
went to Waitrose.

And they bought a very big bag of frozen
chips, in case the teenager should ever
come to tea again.

But he never did…

…or at least not until about an hour later,
when he texted his daddy to tell him,
'I lost my bus pass. Can I have a lift home?'